This Walker book belongs to:

_____

_____

_____

JULIAN AT THE WEDDING

To Danny

First published 2020 by Walker Books Ltd, 87 Vauxhall Walk,
London SE11 5HJ • This edition published 2021 • © 2020 Jessica Love
The moral rights of the author-illustrator have been asserted • This book
has been typeset in Godlike • Printed in China • All rights reserved.
British Library Cataloguing in Publication Data is available
ISBN 978-1-4063-9846-5 • 10 9 8 7 6 5 4 3 2 1

Jessica Love

WALKER BOOKS
AND SUBSIDIARIES
LONDON · BOSTON · SYDNEY · AUCKLAND

This is Julian.

And this is Marisol.

Today they are going to be in a wedding.

Those are the brides, and that's their dog, Gloria.

A wedding is a party for love.

"Let's go," whispers Marisol.

"It's a fairy house," whispers Julian.

"Marisol?"

"Oh."

"Uh-oh!"

Julian has an idea...

"I got dirty."

"Yes, darling, but now you have wings!"

"There you are!"

And then there was dancing.

Praise for *Julian is a Mermaid:*

Winner of the 2019 Klaus Flugge Prize

Winner of the 2019 Stonewall Book Award

Shortlisted for the Waterstone's Children's Book Award

"Readers learn that anyone can be a mermaid. All it takes is love and acceptance, a little imagination, and a big, swishy tail" *The New York Times*

"Celebratory and ground-breaking" *The Sunday Times*

"Utterly gorgeous … great for questioning our gender stereotypes but without being at all preachy" *Sun*

"Fabulous in every sense" *Guardian*

"A lesson in self-love for all ages" *Pride Magazine*

"Beautiful. Magnificent. Magical." *RuPaul*

JULIAN IS A MERMAID

Jessica Love

ISBN 978-1-4063-8642-4